A Turn for Lucas

by Gloria Averbuch

illustrations by Yaacov Guterman

mitten press

All inquiries should be addressed to:

Mitten Press

An imprint of Ann Arbor Media Group LLC

2500 S. State Street

Ann Arbor, MI 48104

Printed and bound in Canada.

10   9   8   7   6   5   4   3   2   1

Library of Congress Cataloging-in-Publication Data

Averbuch, Gloria, 1951-

A turn for Lucas / by Gloria Averbuch ; illustrations by Yaacov Guterman.

p. cm.

Summary: Knowing that he is not as good a soccer player as his sister, Lucas is very
nervous when the coach puts him in as goalie early in a game against the Sharks.

ISBN-13: 978-1-58726-291-3 (hardcover : alk. paper)

ISBN-10: 1-58726-291-6 (hardcover : alk. paper)

[1. Soccer--Fiction. 2. Self-confidence--Fiction. 3. Brothers and sisters--Fiction. 4. Brazilian
Americans--Fiction.] I. Guterman, Ya'akov, ill. II. Title.

PZ7.A93382Tur 2006

[E]--dc22

2005037967

Book design by Somberg Design

www.sombergdesign.com

My twin sister Amelia and I are on a soccer team named the Rebels. I like to go to practice, but Amelia lives for it.

Soccer has always been a part of my life. My mom and dad are from Brazil, where everyone plays the game they call Futebol (foot-tee-bol).

Amelia and I have soccer posters all over our room. Our family talks about our favorite players at dinner. We watch soccer on TV. We go

to Giants Stadium to see the Red Bulls, our local team. In Brazil, you don't just say you cheer for your team. You say, "I am the Red Bulls."

Amelia and I share everything. We split our dessert. Sometimes, Amelia even measures with a ruler to make sure it's fair. We help each other do chores. "Lucas, it's time to set the table," she calls out as she juggles the soccer ball around the kitchen.

Amelia is always tapping the soccer ball up and down on her feet, her thighs, and even her head. When she's not playing, she's thinking about playing. In school, I see her look out the window, longing for recess. On the soccer field, she shouts directions to the other kids. Our coach says she's a natural leader.

"I'm not as good as Amelia," I tell my dad. But he always reminds me, "Lucas, there are all kinds of skills in soccer. All kinds of players. You can be good at different things, for different reasons."

We play games against other teams. It's supposed to be just for fun. But the minute the whistle blows, some of the parents start to yell. That can make the game seem too serious. It sure feels that way today. We're playing the Sharks.

While we're warming up, I hear some of them laughing. "You've got girls on your team," they say.

Their coach gets angry. "I don't want to hear another word," he tells them. "I've seen this team play. If you're not careful, they'll teach you a lesson!"

In the beginning, I have to watch from the bench. But we all get time to play. That's the rule. Josh scores the first goal on a pass from Amelia.

The Sharks are battling back. One of their players is dribbling the ball toward our goal. He takes a good shot. Our goalie dives and saves it from going into the goal. He lands pretty hard. The referee goes over to check on him.

Our coach looks toward the bench and nods his head at me. "Lucas, you're up." I'm confused. Our team practices every position, but I haven't played goalie in a real game. Everyone on the field is standing still, waiting. I look toward Amelia. She gives me our signal: thumbs up in the air. "You can do it," her look says.

Our goalie is carried off. He hands me his special gloves. The coach can see my hands shaking like an earthquake. "It's okay," he tells me, "This is how you learn." I put on the goalie shirt and run onto the field. "The team needs me," I tell myself.

In goal, you have to pay close attention to the game. You can't just take a nap waiting for the ball.

In no time, an army of players is running right at me. A Shark passes a low ball toward the goal. I lean left, but the ball goes right into the net. The Sharks' parents celebrate loud and long.

I take the ball from the back of the net. I glance at my mom in the crowd. What's she doing? She's clapping. "That's okay Lucas. You'll get it next time," she shouts. I try hard not to cry.

I move around to stay warm. The referee blows the whistle and points to the penalty spot. One of the Sharks has tripped our player Suzanna. The Rebels are given a penalty kick. That means it's one against one— a Rebel against the Shark's goalie. The coach chooses Amelia.

My heart kicks against my chest. I'm nervous for her. The whistle blows again. Everyone is quiet. She shoots.

Score! It's our turn to celebrate.

It's 2-1, Rebels. Can we hold on? There isn't much time left. I hope our players keep them back. Just then, a Shark gets the ball. He dribbles by everyone and races toward me. I move out, spreading my arms to protect the goal

Suddenly, the ball is in the air. I freeze.

"Jump!" I hear inside my head. And I do. I feel the tips of my gloves touch the ball, and I hold it there. Safe. My teammates are a field of firecrackers, exploding all around me.

"Lucas!" Amelia yells. I hear her voice over all the others. "Great save!"

We celebrate with ice cream. The Sharks are there too. Everyone seems to forget the score once they get a taste of their favorite flavor. Amelia and I walk to our teammates, balancing our cones—chocolate for her, strawberry with sprinkles for me.

"Great job," a kid from the Shark's table calls out. I turn to Amelia. He must be talking to her. Amelia smiles at me and whispers, "You're a star. You flew to get that ball." I like the idea of flying, reaching the sky to be that star.

Sometimes soccer is hard, especially when some parents and coaches make it that way. Maybe I won't be a star next week, but that's okay. I will still love playing what people all over the world call "the beautiful game."